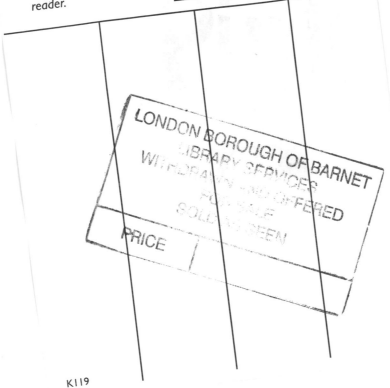

For Hilary – KW

For my dear friend Bianca – BN

First published in 2001 by Macmillan Children's Books
A division of Macmillan Publishers Limited
20 New Wharf Road, London N1 9RR
Basingstoke and Oxford
Associated companies throughout the world
www.panmacmillan.com

ISBN 0 333 90082 0 (HB)
ISBN 0 333 90083 9 (PB)

Text copyright © 2001 Karen Wallace
Illustrations copyright © 2001 Barbara Nascimbeni
Moral rights asserted

1 3 5 7 9 8 6 4 2

A CIP catalogue record for this book is available from the British Library.

Printed in Belgium by Proost.

Archie Hates
Pink

By Karen Wallace

Illustrated by Barbara Nascimbeni

MACMILLAN
CHILDREN'S BOOKS

Archie was a big orange cat. He lived in a
bright white house with a painter called Tallulah.
Every day Tallulah painted lots of pictures.
And every day Archie sat on the window sill
and watched her.

Archie liked most colours.
He liked **blue** because it was the colour of the sky.

He liked **green** because it was the colour of the grass.

He liked **silver** because it was the colour of the
tin opener that opened his cat food.

And he liked **yellow** because it was the colour of his bowl.

There was only one colour that Archie didn't like.
And that colour was **pink**.

Archie hated pink
more than anything
in the whole world.

Archie hated pink
because his stinky
flea powder was
in a pink bottle.

He hated pink because
his brush with the prickly
bristles had a pink handle.

He especially hated pink
because the horrible medicine
he sometimes had to swallow
was always pink.

One day a terrible thing happened. Tallulah stopped painting pictures. She got out a ladder, she picked up a huge roller. And she began to paint the house pink!

"How could she?" yowled Archie to his best friend Max. "I'm leaving home and I'm never coming back!" And even though Tallulah called him and called him, Archie pretended he couldn't hear her.

"It's time you learned a few things,"
said Max. Max was a mysterious cat.
Nobody knew where Max came from
and nobody asked. But there was nothing
Max didn't know.

Max took Archie
to the market.
Archie had never been
to a market before.
He saw loaves of bread
that looked like birds.

He saw baskets shaped like boats full of flowers. And he saw piles and piles of delicious things to eat.

First they went to a fruit stall. Max pointed to a watermelon. "Watch," he said. As Max spoke a man in a white coat picked up a sharp knife. Whack! He split the watermelon in half!

Archie gasped. Inside it was pink! The kind of bright rosy pink you only see in sunsets.

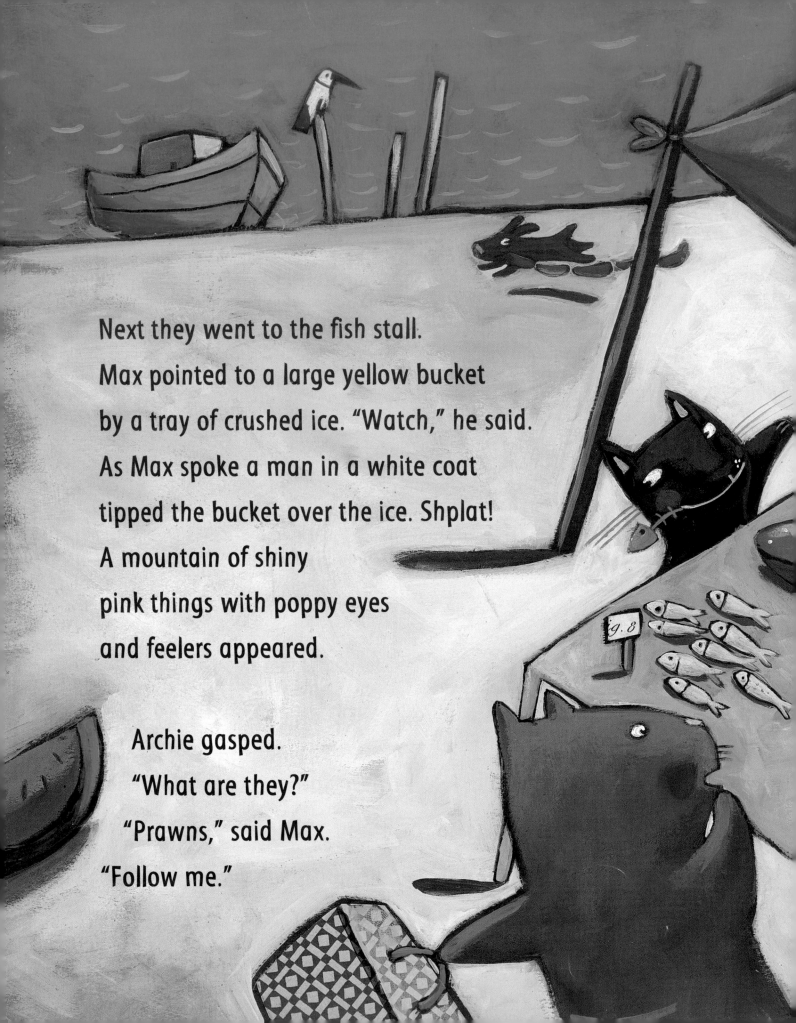

Next they went to the fish stall.
Max pointed to a large yellow bucket
by a tray of crushed ice. "Watch," he said.
As Max spoke a man in a white coat
tipped the bucket over the ice. Shplat!
A mountain of shiny
pink things with poppy eyes
and feelers appeared.

Archie gasped.
"What are they?"
"Prawns," said Max.
"Follow me."

Around the back there was a huge dustbin.
Max jumped in and threw pieces of pink prawns
on the ground. Archie gobbled them up.
They were absolutely delicious!

On the way home, Archie saw a man selling carnations. They were pink and pretty with frilly edges. He crept nearer. They smelled like Tallulah's favourite perfume.

Archie thought of how Tallulah had called and called and he had pretended not to hear. He thought of all the kind things Tallulah did for him.

It wasn't her fault the flea powder bottle was pink.

Or the prickly brush had a pink handle.

Or the horrible cat medicine
was pink.

Suddenly Archie wanted to say he was sorry
for being such a silly spoilt cat.

Max watched Archie carefully through narrow eyes.

It was almost as if he knew what Archie was thinking.

"Say it with flowers," purred Max.

So Archie grabbed a mouthful of carnations and ran

down the road. Tallulah was sitting sadly on the grass.

Behind her the house sparkled with pink paint.

Archie couldn't believe his eyes. It was the sort of pink that made you dream of delicious fish. It was the sort of pink you only see in sunsets.

"Max," he cried. "I love pink and it's all because of you!"

But Max had disappeared.

And Tallulah was running
across the grass.

And holding out her arms.

ALSO PUBLISHED BY MACMILLAN:

Small Brown Dog's Bad Remembering Day

by Mike Gibbie, illustrated by Barbara Nascimbeni

Madeleine the City Pig

by Karen Wallace, illustrated by Lydia Monks

Esmerelda

by Karen Wallace, illustrated by Lydia Monks

MACMILLAN CHILDREN'S BOOKS